The Edge of Tomorrow

The Edge of Tomorrow

A Journey of Self-Discovery

Elias Hartley

RWG Publishing

Contents

1   Chapter 1: The Ordinary Beginning   1

2   Chapter 2: The Unexpected Catalyst   5

3   Chapter 3: The Call to Adventure   12

4   Chapter 4: The Labyrinth of Reflections   18

5   Chapter 5: The Symphony of Choices   25

6   Chapter 6: The Canvas of Tomorrow   32

7   Chapter 7: The Symphony of Choices   39

8   Chapter 8: The Cosmic Echoes   49

9   Chapter 9: Whispers of Destiny   57

10   Chapter 10: The Tapestry Unveiled   65

11   Chapter 11: The Celestial Reckoning   73

12   Chapter 12: The Celestial Genesis   80

Copyright © 2024 by Elias Hartley

All rights reserved. No part of this book may be reproduced in any manner whatsoever without written permission except in the case of brief quotations embodied in critical articles and reviews.

First Printing, 2024

{ **1** }

Chapter 1: The Ordinary Beginning

The alarm clock abruptly awakened Alex Turner, its persistent beeping slicing through the mundane morning. Alex rubbed the sleep from their eyes and swung their legs over the bed's edge, feet touching the cool hardwood floor of the small-town apartment. Ahead lay another day marked by the same monotonous rhythm, reflecting the town's predictable nature.

As the scent of brewing coffee filled the air, Alex moved through the morning rituals mechanically. The kitchen, a testament to daily routines, had witnessed countless solitary breakfasts. The local bookstore, where Alex worked, beckoned—a place where days merged indistinguishably among dusty shelves and aged novels.

Morning sunlight streamed through curtained windows, casting a warm glow in the room. Despite this, Alex couldn't shake a feeling of unease, a subtle whisper of something amiss. With keys in hand, they locked the door and stepped onto the cobblestone sidewalk. The town, with its familiar faces and facades, embraced the ordinary, yet today, it carried a hint of impending change.

Walking past the usual sights—the local diner, the weathered park bench—the town's rhythm felt reassuring. However, under the surface, a tension simmered, hinting at the unexpected just around the corner. The day unfolded like many others, but unbeknownst to Alex, it held the seeds of an extraordinary journey, beginning with the ring of the bookstore's bell—a call to adventure that would break the monotony and alter Alex's life.

The bookstore, a haven of familiar tales, welcomed Alex with the soft jingle of its creaky door. The smell of old paper and ink usually provided solace, but today, the air buzzed with a charged energy. Alex carried out their tasks, shelving books and aiding customers, but the day's odd occurrence lingered in their mind.

As evening approached, Alex noticed a peculiar tome in a forgotten store corner. Dust swirled in the fading sunlight as they touched the book's spine. The atmosphere shifted; a resonance emanated from the ancient book, hinting at hidden mysteries.

The book fell open, revealing cryptic symbols and an unfamiliar yet oddly recognizable language. The words seemed to rearrange themselves, conveying a message meant for Alex. Realization struck: the day's events, the mysterious book, all were intertwined, marking the start of a journey into the unknown.

The Edge of Tomorrow

After closing, the bookstore, shadow-filled and silent, beckoned Alex back to the enigmatic book. They felt a shift, a change in the air, as they sat at a desk, re-opening the book. The symbols glowed faintly, the language stirring a deep familiarity. Questions and anticipation swirled in Alex's mind. What was this book's significance? How did it connect to the day's strange beginning?

The implications of the day's events became apparent, revealing a heightened awareness of the world. The once monotonous town now held secrets and potential revelations. Faced with a choice—to delve into these mysteries or return to comfort—Alex contemplated their path. The ordinary had given way to the extraordinary.

The next morning brought a sense of anticipation. The town seemed expectant as a mysterious figure, central to the day's events, appeared. In the bookstore, where secrets whispered from book pages, this guide revealed a hidden aspect of Alex's identity.

"I've been expecting you," the figure said, their voice blending assurance and mystery. They connected the peculiar morning, the mysterious book, and the journey ahead. Alex faced a decision: remain in the familiar or embrace the extraordinary and embark on a journey of self-discovery.

Choosing to follow the guide, Alex stepped into a new world. The town's ordinary backdrop transformed into a landscape of symbols and meanings. Every interaction mirrored aspects of Alex's story, forming deep connections and hinting at a larger destiny.

The guide, a mentor, revealed wisdom and purpose,

awakening Alex to their intertwined destiny. As the journey peaked, Alex approached a turning point, ready to embrace their full identity and the limitless possibilities of self-discovery.

{ 2 }

Chapter 2: The Unexpected Catalyst

As the sun dipped low on the horizon, long shadows stretched across the town square where Alex stood, their mind still echoing with the morning's peculiar events. The air thrummed with anticipation, as if it was laden with secrets yet to unfold.

In the dimming light, a mysterious figure emerged from the shadows, their silhouette etched against the fading daylight. Draped in an aura of mystery and intent, they approached Alex with a serene confidence, as though destiny had orchestrated this meeting since time's inception.

"Alex Turner," the guide spoke, their voice imbued with ancient wisdom, "the ordinary is but a veil over the extraordinary. Your journey is just beginning."

A mix of curiosity and apprehension fluttered in Alex's chest. The guide, their eyes seemingly holding centuries of knowledge, extended a hand to reveal an object—a key, an amulet, a relic of unknown origins. Its significance hung in the air like a tacit promise.

"Yesterday's events were not mere coincidence," the guide continued, their voice weaving a tapestry of revelation. "They were the initial notes in a symphony that resonates with the essence of your being."

In the quiet of the town square, as daylight gave way to night, Alex felt an invisible thread binding them to the guide, intertwining their fates in destiny's vast tapestry. This encounter was more than a crossing of paths; it was the catalyst for a journey that would transcend the ordinary—a voyage of self-discovery, guided by forces beyond understanding.

The room, lit only by a lone lamp, offered Alex refuge from the day's enigmatic events. As they pondered the object, it shimmered with a transcendent light. A surge of awareness flowed through Alex, awakening senses that had lain dormant. The once mundane room transformed into a haven of hidden symbols and ethereal energies.

The guide, now a spectral presence in the half-light, stood beside Alex, offering reassurance amidst the unfolding mystery. They began to unveil ancient wisdom hidden within the ordinary. "Perception is but a veil," the guide intoned, their words echoing across time. Symbols around them glowed with newfound meaning, unveiling a narrative woven into existence itself.

As the lessons deepened, Alex's senses sharpened. The air carried whispers of secrets, the walls spoke of forgotten tales, and the ground seemed alive with the pulse of a hidden world. This awakening was both thrilling and unsettling—a collision of the known and the unknown.

Yet, doubt crept into Alex's mind. At the edge of acceptance, they wrestled with the enormity of their new awareness. Sensing Alex's inner conflict, the guide offered encouragement, sharing tales of others who had embarked on similar journeys—stories of triumph and transformation awaiting those who embraced the extraordinary.

In the room's quietude, with the mysterious object as a beacon and the guide as a custodian of ancient truths, Alex faced a crossroads. The familiar world beckoned, but the extraordinary called, promising a journey beyond the mundane. It was a hesitant acceptance, a yielding to destiny's pull—a choice made in the fleeting moments when the worlds of the ordinary and extraordinary intertwined into a tapestry of infinite possibilities.

The next day dawned with Alex wrestling with reluctance. The guide's revelations echoed persistently, demanding recognition. The sun's golden rays over the town underscored the weight of the extraordinary that Alex was hesitant to fully embrace.

At home, the cryptic object sat on a table, a silent testament to the impending journey. Doubt lingered in Alex's mind, advocating for the safety of the familiar. Yet, the guide, attuned to Alex's turmoil, returned with a blend of comfort and resolve. "The journey is a dance between doubt and faith," they said, their words soothing Alex's inner chaos.

As the guide recounted stories of others who had faced similar crossroads, their words became a lifeline for Alex.

These narratives of overcoming doubt and weaving destinies into existence's tapestry resonated deeply.

Gradually, Alex began to embrace the reality beyond the ordinary. The guide's words eroded their doubts, planting seeds of possibility. This decision to embark on the journey was a conscious leap beyond comfort, a commitment to exploring uncharted aspects of the self.

The room, once a haven of hesitation, became a cocoon of transformation. The guide, a beacon of wisdom, imparted lessons on inner strength and resilience. Each story reinforced the innate potential for growth and the boundless spirit within.

With a reluctant nod, Alex acknowledged the necessity of the journey. The guide prepared to lead them from the known to the realms of self-discovery. As the door creaked open to the morning-lit town, Alex stepped into a corridor of uncertainty. The journey had begun—a pilgrimage into the soul's uncharted landscapes, guided by wisdom and fueled by the stories of those who had emerged transformed from the edge of doubt.

In the morning-lit town square, Alex, accompanied by the steadfast guide, faced the choice between the ordinary and the extraordinary. Taking a deep breath, Alex decided to step beyond the familiar, venturing into a realm where reality intertwined with destiny's threads. The guide nodded, as if this choice was preordained.

As they walked, the town's boundaries dissolved, revealing a surreal landscape pulsating with ancient energies. This

The Edge of Tomorrow

transition was both physical and metaphysical, a passage into a dimension where reality's rules were redefined.

The guide, a guardian of the extraordinary, continued to unravel this new realm's mysteries. They spoke of universal interconnectedness, the flow of energies, and the balance of existence. Alex, once a mere observer, now absorbed this wisdom, each step deepening their understanding.

Symbols, once enigmatic, became clear. The mysterious object in Alex's possession became a guide, leading them through self-discovery's uncharted territories. The landscape unfolded like a narrative, with the guide sharing their own journey of challenges and victories, doubts and eventual acceptance of destiny.

As they ventured further, time and space blurred, reality responding to their intentions and awareness. Alex, liberated from ordinary constraints, moved with transcendent fluidity.

Each revelation expanded Alex's understanding of their identity. This journey wasn't just an external exploration but a deep dive into the self, unearthing hidden potentials and capacities.

The chapter concluded with Alex at the known and unknown intersection, a symbol of potential in the uncharted landscape. The guide, acknowledging their progress, pointed towards the horizon, where further experiences and revelations awaited. The ordinary world, now a memory, gave way to the extraordinary—a realm where the self merged into infinite possibilities.

The uncharted landscape sprawled before Alex, a

kaleidoscope beyond the familiar spectrum. The guide, a figure against this ethereal backdrop, beckoned towards the horizon, the next journey's chapter.

Stepping into the unknown, the air vibrated with anticipation. The guide's teachings, now part of Alex's essence, led them towards self-discovery's core.

The ever-shifting landscape mirrored Alex's inner journey. Each step became a meditation, exploring their untapped potential. The guide, a constant, revealed the synergy between traveler and uncharted realms.

Symbols, celestial and earthly, became waypoints in this cosmic pilgrimage. The mysterious object, a channel for wisdom, guided Alex through the revelations.

The journey, marked by challenges and victories, tested Alex's resilience and newfound strength. The surreal landscape mirrored their internal struggles and successes.

With each obstacle surmounted, Alex's perception of reality broadened. The guide, now more than a mentor, reflected the boundless possibilities within.

In moments of cosmic contemplation, the guide shared timeless lessons, clarifying the journey's purpose—an unmasking of the self to discover core truths hidden by the ordinary's veils.

Venturing deeper, Alex felt a profound connection to existence itself. The line between self and surroundings blurred, merging into the cosmic tapestry.

The chapter closed with Alex at revelation's brink, the guide hinting at further mysteries. The ordinary, now a past

The Edge of Tomorrow

echo, had given way to a transformative odyssey—a self-exploration extending beyond perception's edges.

The journey continued, a self-discovery symphony against the extraordinary backdrop. With the guide leading, the uncharted landscape promised infinite possibilities, beckoning Alex to a horizon where the once-ordinary self stood on the brink of limitless potential.

Chapter 3: The Call to Adventure

In the silent expanse of the uncharted landscape, Alex delved into the reverberations of their family history. The guide, wise and ancient, began to unravel a hidden tapestry of secrets, untold stories, and a lineage that intertwined Alex with the cosmic dance of existence.

Beside a glowing stream, whispering with ancestral voices, the guide spoke of blood ties and wisdom passed through generations. The unfolding legacy revealed not only the struggles and triumphs of Alex's ancestors but also the profound purpose woven into Alex's own being.

As the guide's narrative unfolded, the landscape transformed, bringing to life ancestral scenes of hardship, victory, and sacrifice. Alex, now the bearer of this familial tale, felt a deep responsibility, recognizing their personal journey as inseparably linked to these unresolved histories.

A mix of pride, awe, and melancholy swept through Alex,

The Edge of Tomorrow

acknowledging the weight carried by their forebears. The guide's words bridged past and present, intertwining Alex's identity with the threads of history woven into the cosmos's fabric.

With this new awareness, Alex grappled with merging their ordinary past life with the extraordinary legacy now revealed. The murmuring stream reflected this inner struggle, a symbol of the complex interplay between personal choice and destiny's currents.

Sensing Alex's emotional turmoil, the guide offered quiet reassurance. They emphasized the continuum of self-discovery, where past, present, and future merge in a seamless dance, affirming life's intricate patterns.

By the luminous stream, Alex stood at the confluence of their history, custodian of a legacy transcending time. The mysteries of the past became guideposts on their journey, where each ancestral story lit the way towards self-discovery.

In the uncharted landscape's heart, Alex faced a symbolic ordeal, a rite of passage sculpting their path to self-realization. The guide, a silent observer, watched as Alex confronted challenges that tested their abilities and essence.

The environment mirrored Alex's inner world, presenting tangible and metaphysical hurdles—manifestations of fears and doubts. The guide's encouraging voice urged Alex to trust their inner strength.

Each trial reflected Alex's internal landscape. The first challenge, embodying fear, forced Alex to face peripheral shadows of their consciousness. The guide's words fortified Alex against self-doubt and uncertainty.

Next, a labyrinth of choices emerged, symbolizing life's intricate decisions. The guide's voice guided Alex to the maze's heart, where their true self awaited revelation.

Each obstacle, a confrontation with inner shadows, required intuition and newfound abilities. This symbolic test mirrored the broader self-discovery journey, navigating self-complexities to emerge transformed.

The guide's presence offered solace as Alex traversed the labyrinth. Their encouragement and the responsive environment bolstered Alex's resolve. This crucible of growth honed Alex's understanding of their capabilities.

At the labyrinth's center, Alex emerged as a symbol of resilience and awareness. The guide's approving nod signaled the journey's continuation, with the test marking both personal triumph and a shift in Alex's self-narrative.

In the mystical realm, Alex encountered various beings. The guide explained the nature of these interactions: some allies, others adversaries, each playing a role in Alex's self-discovery.

An ethereal being of light and wisdom taught Alex cosmic interconnectedness. The guide highlighted the significance of such allies, reflecting qualities Alex sought within.

Yet, not all encounters were peaceful. Emerging shadows, representing fears and conflicts, provided growth opportunities. The guide supported Alex in confronting these adversaries, turning conflicts into catalysts for evolution.

These encounters mirrored human connection complexities. Some beings became trusted companions; others, transient lessons in Alex's journey. The guide elucidated the deeper meaning of each relationship, revealing allies as keys to unlocking potential and adversaries as mirrors for internal reconciliation.

Each encounter enriched Alex's journey, weaving a tapestry of experiences that illuminated the path of self-discovery. The guide, with foresight, led Alex towards the journey's next phase, hinting at the myriad possibilities in the uncharted realms.

At the celestial pool, the guide linked Alex's past to their current odyssey. Through symbols and stories, they stressed resolving past issues for true self-discovery.

Scenes from Alex's life materialized, each a piece of their life's puzzle. Childhood memories, decisions, and relationships all played a role in shaping Alex's identity.

The pool reflected both joyful moments and underlying shadows. The guide helped Alex navigate memory's labyrinth, illuminating each moment's significance in their identity formation.

Alex saw how past choices intertwined with consequences, realizing self-discovery intertwines past, present, and future. The guide, well-versed in cosmic narratives, highlighted resolution's power in bridging past fragments with future possibilities.

At the pool, Alex confronted unresolved emotions. The guide offered steady support, encouraging Alex to face memory's shadows. Each revelation was a step towards deeper self-understanding, a reconciliation process resonating with life's ancient rhythms.

As past scenes unfolded, Alex stood at the junction of

history and destiny. The guide hinted at transformation through resolution—a key to unlocking self-discovery's doors.

With clarity, Alex recognized confronting their past's unresolved aspects was vital. The pool, a history and potential mirror, rippled with Alex's decision to reshape their past as part of their self-discovery journey. The guide led forward, with Alex poised for transformative revelations in the unexplored self realms.

After the celestial pool revelation, Alex prepared to confront memory's shadows. The guide, steadfast, led them towards this crucial self-discovery moment.

A shadowy figure from Alex's past appeared, embodying unresolved emotions and truths. The guide stood by, a silent witness to the confrontation.

The encounter was a blend of past and present, with old wounds echoing in the air. The shadowy figure prompted Alex to address long-buried emotions shaping their self-perception.

The guide's steady voice encouraged Alex to confront the shadows bravely. In this timeless landscape, Alex faced a reckoning, redefining their past narrative and future foundation.

Emotions surged as Alex confronted the figure, releasing long-suppressed anger and pain. The guide's empathetic presence helped Alex navigate this emotional upheaval.

The confrontation became a transformative crucible. In facing the shadows, Alex found the strength to voice unspoken truths, facilitated by the guide's unwavering support.

With each acknowledgment, the shadows dissipated,

The Edge of Tomorrow

transforming the landscape into a healing space. The guide observed the cathartic release, marking the resolution of a significant life chapter.

As the figure dissolved, Alex felt liberated, a lightness permeating the landscape. The guide's affirmative nod signaled progress—a release from the past and a step towards self-awareness.

Moving forward, the landscape seemed to exhale, releasing the emotional storm's echoes. The guide, accompanying Alex, hinted at the horizon's vast possibilities.

The chapter concluded with Alex, freed from past burdens, on the brink of a new beginning. The transformed landscape beckoned them forward, its echoes guiding the ongoing self-discovery symphony.

{ 4 }

Chapter 4: The Labyrinth of Reflections

In the heart of the uncharted landscape, where the air buzzed with the secrets of hidden wonders, Alex discovered a seemingly mundane mirror. Yet, upon gazing into it, they sensed its magic—a portal to realms beyond the physical.

The guide, attuned to the landscape's arcane energies, led Alex to the mirror. Its frame, adorned with shimmering, ethereal symbols, beckoned Alex closer with its mysterious allure.

"This mirror," the guide elucidated, "reflects more than your physical form. It's a gateway to your thoughts and emotions, a key to the mysteries beneath your surface."

With a mix of hesitation and curiosity, Alex approached the enchanted mirror. Their reflection gave way to a swirling kaleidoscope of images, transcending time. Memories, desires, and fears played out in a surreal display, mirroring Alex's complex inner self.

The Edge of Tomorrow

The guide's calming voice guided Alex through this reflective maze. "What you see is your soul's tapestry, a mosaic of experiences. Embrace each image; they form the fabric of your identity."

Delving deeper, Alex gained profound self-awareness. The mirror revealed not just the past, but also the present—the thoughts and emotions weaving through their consciousness.

However, darker shades emerged. Shadows of unresolved traumas and buried regrets surfaced, transforming the mirror into a gateway to inner darkness, demanding a brave confrontation.

The guide, steadfast by Alex's side, offered compassionate advice. "True self-knowledge involves embracing all aspects of oneself. Face these inner demons with kindness, as you would with a close friend."

In this reflective dance, a critical moment of self-healing unfolded. Armed with insight, Alex navigated this emotional landscape with vulnerability and resilience. The mirror served as a conduit to the soul's depths, facilitating a cathartic transformation that brought Alex to the brink of inner clarity.

As this scene closed, the guide nodded towards the journey's next phase. The mirror, having revealed Alex's layered self, stood as a symbol of the transformative power of self-awareness—an enchanted gateway leading to the uncharted landscapes of tomorrow.

Echoes of the guide's words still hanging in the air, Alex revisited the mirror with newfound determination. The reflective surface now seemed a familiar path to self-discovery.

Alex saw a dance of colors and forms within the mirror—a kaleidoscope that went beyond the physical. Memories emerged, weaving into the display's intricate patterns. Desires and fears also surfaced, casting their shadows on this reflective canvas.

The guide encouraged Alex to embrace the complexity of these reflections. "This kaleidoscope holds your essence. Each image, a chapter of your story, adds to your existence's tapestry. Acknowledge them as part of your cosmic symphony."

Immersed in the subconscious labyrinth, Alex experienced a blend of thoughts and emotions. The guide's gentle wisdom helped decipher the symbolic language of these reflections.

The mirror now reflected both past and present, exposing the thoughts and feelings within Alex's heart. It was a revelation of self-awareness beyond ordinary introspection.

Yet, as the reflections deepened, so did the shadows. Darker hues signaled unresolved traumas and hidden regrets—challenging aspects of Alex's psyche that needed acknowledgment.

The guide, ever supportive, counseled Alex. "To confront these shadows is to reclaim parts of yourself. This journey through darker reflections is a path to healing and integration."

In this space of self-confrontation, Alex faced their inner demons. The labyrinth became a crucible for self-discovery. Each confronted shadow rippled through the reflective surface, echoing transformation.

As the scene reached its climax, the guide acknowledged Alex's bravery. The mirror, having revealed the soul's

The Edge of Tomorrow

intricacies, became a profound testament to the uncharted landscapes beneath the familiar surface. The journey, while challenging, turned into a pilgrimage into the self's heart, guided by the mirror's ethereal light.

Emerging from the intricate revelations within the enchanted mirror, Alex stood ready to confront their psyche's darker recesses. The labyrinth of reflections, now fully unveiled, became an emotional crucible.

The guide, a beacon amidst these shadows, accompanied Alex as the mirror's surface rippled with echoes of unresolved traumas and regrets. Each shadow, a symbol of past wounds, called for acknowledgment and healing.

The guide's melodic words guided Alex through this emotional terrain. The reflections, now somber, mirrored the human experience's complexities, urging Alex to confront the shadows with compassion.

Each reflection, born of past pain, became a step toward understanding. The guide's steady presence reassured Alex that this journey was a shared human experience.

Facing forgotten traumas and regrets, Alex navigated the emotional landscape. The mirror became a window to their deepest struggles, requiring vulnerability and resilience for transformation.

The guide, sensing the energy shifts, offered insights and encouragement. "Confronting these shadows reclaims power over your past. Acknowledging these aspects paves the way for a future free from unresolved emotions."

As Alex moved through the labyrinth, their courage and compassion reshaped the reflective surface. The emotional release transformed the landscape, marking the journey with resilience and healing.

The labyrinth, though intricate, now bore signs of healing. The guide nodded towards the journey's next stage. The mirror, having served as a soul portal, stood as a testament to embracing one's shadows. Alex stepped away, ready to continue their exploration of the uncharted landscape with newfound clarity and purpose.

At the enchanted mirror's heart, Alex faced prophetic displays—a glimpse into potential futures. The guide, an interpreter of cosmic tales, accompanied Alex as the mirror revealed scenes of destinies intertwined with choices yet to be made.

Alex, now aware of the weight of each decision, watched the unfolding destinies with a mix of hope and apprehension. The guide offered insight into each prophetic image, highlighting the continuous dance with destiny that marks a journey of self-discovery.

The reflections showcased various potential paths, some radiant with success, others shrouded in uncertainty. The guide narrated these timelines, providing context to the tapestry of futures.

The mirror not only foretold external events but also the evolution of Alex's character. The guide emphasized the transformative impact of each decision, affecting the identity's very fabric.

Alex stood at a crossroads, contemplating the balance between free will and cosmic guidance. The guide's wisdom illuminated each prophetic image, guiding Alex towards their unfolding future.

As the final reflection faded, the guide reminded Alex that the true artistry lies in their choices. The journey of self-discovery is shaped by intentions and decisions springing from the self's core.

With these revelations in mind, Alex approached the mirror's edge. The guide, a companion in destiny's dance, pointed towards the uncharted horizon. The mirror, now an oracle and reflection, became a compass for the journey ahead.

Stepping away from the mirror, Alex faced a decision-laden path. The guide reminded them that their journey's essence lies in their choices. Each step is a stroke on destiny's canvas.

In the uncharted landscape's quiet expanse, Alex pondered the emotional revelations and prophetic glimpses of future paths. The guide's words, echoing through the stillness, encouraged Alex to embrace uncertainty as the canvas for their life's masterpiece.

Taking the first step into their journey's unfolding chapters, Alex ventured into the mysterious landscape. The guide, a spiritual companion, walked alongside, embodying the journey's ever-evolving nature.

As the scene faded, the mirror's echoes remained imprinted on Alex's soul. The edge of tomorrow beckoned, promising a symphony of experiences, choices, and discoveries—a landscape where the extraordinary emerged from the ordinary, and each step echoed with infinite possibilities on the horizon.

{ 5 }

Chapter 5: The Symphony of Choices

At the crossroads of destiny, Alex paused in contemplation. The profound revelations of the enchanted mirror cast long shadows over the junction where diverging paths invited exploration. The guide, a wise presence, offered insights into the nuances of decision-making.

"The crossroads," began the guide, "is where the symphony of your intentions takes shape. Each choice resonates within the corridors of destiny, with your intentions weaving through the fabric of the unknown like threads."

The air at the crossroads vibrated with cosmic energies, and Alex felt the burden of their newfound self-awareness. The once obscure choices, hidden behind the veil of the future, now appeared clear, each with the potential to shape their life's narrative.

With the guide's words resonating, Alex surveyed the diverging paths—a labyrinth of possibilities stretching into the uncharted. The reflections from the mirror, still vivid in their mind, served as a compass through this complex web of intentions.

The guide spoke of the importance of deliberate choice. "Your intentions are the silent architects of your destiny. Choose with clarity and authenticity, for each decision sculpts the journey ahead."

The crossroads became a theater for introspection. Equipped with insights from the mirror and guided by the sage's wisdom, Alex grappled with the responsibility that comes with conscious choice. This intersection, a melting pot of past, present, and potential futures, was ripe with transformative possibilities.

Alex took their first step towards a chosen path with quiet determination. The guide, observing this pivotal moment, nodded in approval. The crossroads, more than a metaphor, was a sacred space where the whispers of intention met the currents of destiny.

As Alex proceeded, the uncharted landscape welcomed them, their symphony of choices resonating melodically. The guide, now a fellow traveler in Alex's narrative of self-discovery, walked alongside, a guardian of crossroads and a custodian of intentions.

The scene closed with Alex, having embarked on a chosen path, venturing into the unknown. The subtle harmonies of their intentions lingered in the air, becoming part of the continuous symphony of choices. The guide, with a knowing look, hinted at the endless possibilities awaiting on this new path—the canvas of destiny being painted with the brush of conscious choice.

Deep in the uncharted landscape, cosmic currents guided Alex to a place of serenity. The whispering breeze, both timeless and ethereal, carried stories and latent potentials.

The guide, sensitive to the energies of these realms, led Alex to a tranquil glade. Here, the breeze seemed to carry cosmic secrets, with leaves rustling in a chorus of guidance about the looming choices.

"The whispering breeze is the cosmic currents' voice—an oracle revealing the nuances of your choices. Listen closely, for these whispers align intention with destiny," the guide explained.

In the glade's heart, the breeze enveloped Alex in a gentle embrace. The guide urged them to tune into this cosmic symphony, interpreting the air's subtle vibrations.

The breeze, whispering tales from distant worlds and epochs, communicated in a language beyond words. Each rustle offered insights into aligning intention with destiny.

Catching a fleeting breeze, the guide said, "These whispers carry potential futures' energies. Feel them and let them guide you to the path that resonates with your truest self."

Surrendering to the whispers, Alex found peace. The breeze became a cosmic mentor, offering wisdom and echoing the choices ahead, weaving a tapestry of intention and destiny.

In the cosmic energy dance, Alex attuned to the breeze's vibrations. The guide interpreted these cues, aiding Alex in aligning their intentions with cosmic harmonies.

The scene, dreamlike, was a communion with unseen forces guiding the journey. As the whispers faded, the guide smiled, signaling the next odyssey phase. The breeze, now a celestial mentor, guided the ongoing symphony of choices through the uncharted realms.

In the uncharted landscape, Alex's journey wove serendipity into its fabric—a cosmic waltz where chance encounters added complexity. The guide, understanding fate's interconnected threads, illuminated serendipity's role in self-discovery.

In a glade of ancient trees, Alex met a mysterious figure. This chance meeting, orchestrated by destiny, held deep significance.

The guide recognized the serendipitous moment, encouraging Alex to see the encounter's importance. "Serendipity aligns with your journey. These chance meetings hold hidden messages and lessons," they said.

The meeting with the traveler brought shared stories and common fate threads, transcending mere coincidence. The guide allowed this serendipitous dance to unfold naturally.

In their exchange, Alex and the stranger shared experiences and stories, revealing a shared cosmic narrative. The guide, observing, shared insights on recognizing serendipity's patterns.

The glade became a narrative convergence point—a place where individual journeys intersected in the vast uncharted landscape. The stranger added a unique dimension to Alex's symphony of choices.

The guide highlighted serendipitous encounters' transformative power. "Each meeting is part of existence's interconnected web. Embrace synchronicities for insights into your journey," they advised.

As the encounter climaxed, Alex and the stranger parted, their stories entwined in the cosmic saga. The guide prompted Alex to reflect on this serendipitous chapter, a significant piece of their self-discovery narrative.

The glade, now echoing with shared tales, became sacred—a testament to serendipity's profound meaning. The guide gestured towards the uncharted horizon, marking a momentary pause in the journey that left a lasting impact—an intricate design revealing life's interconnectedness.

In the mystical landscape, Alex faced the symbolic veil of uncertainty, accompanied by the guide. This shimmering barrier, rippling with unknown energies, represented the inherent unpredictability of life's choices.

The veil, spanning the path like a cosmic gate, held transformative potential. "Beyond lies the unknown," the guide explained. "Stepping into uncertainty embraces transformation."

Approaching the veil, Alex felt a mix of fear and wonder. The threads of intention from the crossroads, now facing a supreme test, prepared them to embrace the unknown's enigmatic forces.

The guide encouraged Alex to move forward bravely. "Uncertainty is where the universe's masterpieces are painted. Embrace the unknown for self-discovery's magic."

Crossing the veil, Alex entered a dreamscape where reality blurred. The guide's voice remained a constant, leading them through this surreal world, imparting wisdom on navigating shifting landscapes.

The veil marked a transition from the familiar to the extraordinary. Guided by intention and serendipity, Alex ventured deeper into unknown territories, where each step promised revelation.

In this surreal realm, the veil transformed from a barrier to a gateway, opening up infinite possibilities. The guide, understanding, signaled the continuing journey—a path where uncertainty wasn't an obstacle but a sacred route to self-discovery.

As Alex progressed, the echoes of uncertainty danced around them. The guide, a companion in this narrative, reminded them that traversing uncertainty was a harmonious exploration of destiny-shaping cosmic forces.

At destiny's edge, Alex reflected on their journey through the uncharted landscape, the crossroads, the cosmic breeze, chance encounters, and the veil of uncertainty. The choices made and intentions set shaped this chapter in their journey of self-discovery.

The vast landscape spread before them, a canvas of experiences. The guide, observing this transformative journey, pointed to a panoramic view—a display of the cosmic interplay.

Gazing across the horizon, Alex heard the guide speak of the journey's echoes, shaping their destiny. "Destiny is shaped by choices and cosmic forces. Your journey's echoes will resonate through time."

As the cosmic symphony's final notes played, Alex felt

The Edge of Tomorrow

gratitude for the guide's companionship through unknown realms. The journey, filled with challenges and uncertainties, became a self-discovery pilgrimage, where the extraordinary emerged from the ordinary.

In the landscape's ethereal light, Alex prepared for the next narrative steps. The guide offered one last piece of wisdom. "The journey continues. Each chapter delves deeper into self-mysteries. Embrace destiny's echoes and your choice symphony. Your existence's canvas is ever-expanding."

Acknowledging the guide, Alex turned towards the horizon. The guide, now a spiritual guardian, would continue to resonate in the self-discovery echoes.

As the scene faded into the vast expanse, the guide's voice echoed like a cosmic wind whisper. Tomorrow's edge, now within reach, promised an ongoing symphony—an intricate destiny dance where each choice echoed through the uncharted realms, weaving the self-discovery narrative in the cosmic tapestry.

{ 6 }

Chapter 6: The Canvas of Tomorrow

At the cosmic overlook, Alex paused for reflection, absorbing the journey's past echoes and gleaning wisdom for the unfolding chapters. Below lay the uncharted realms, a dance of cosmic energies shimmering in the distance.

The guide, a spectral presence carried by cosmic winds, spoke of reflection's transformative power. "This overlook," they whispered, "harmonizes your journey's echoes with the cosmic symphony. Reflect here, where the canvas of tomorrow gains clarity."

Gazing into the expanse, Alex recalled the crossroads, the whispering breeze, and the veil of uncertainty, each a fragment of a dream. The guide, with timeless serenity, guided Alex in discerning these echoes, each a brushstroke on self-discovery's canvas.

Carried by cosmic winds, echoes of the past fortified Alex for the next chapter. The guide's voice, a gentle current in the cosmic stream, reminded Alex of the intentions woven into their being.

In this pause, the landscape below shimmered with potential. The guide, though unseen, remained a guardian of cosmic wisdom, accompanying Alex's silent meditation on tomorrow's canvas.

Embracing this pause, Alex felt gratitude. The overlook, more than a vantage point, became a sacred space where past echoes met future anticipation. Tomorrow's canvas awaited, ready for the heart's intentions to be painted in vibrant strokes.

With a final look at the cosmic expanse, Alex left the overlook. Accompanied by the guide, a cosmic wind specter, they descended into the cosmic forge, ready to shape intentions for tomorrow's unwritten chapters.

In the celestial forge, where intentions materialize, Alex found an atmosphere charged with potential energy. The guide, a subtle presence, revealed the forge's secrets.

Manifesting as a cosmic atelier, the forge transformed thoughts and intentions into destiny's building blocks. The guide invited Alex to craft intentions, echoing through the astral realm, "Here, thoughts and intentions form destiny's foundation. Each creation is your conscious manifestation's artistry."

Immersed, Alex found the forge responding to their intentions. Ethereal energy sparks illuminated unseen forces, turning thoughts and intentions into reality's tangible threads.

The guide, in tune with creative energy, highlighted the power of conscious creation. "In the forge, you are both artist and masterpiece, shaping the narrative of self-discovery with each intention."

Alex, purposefully crafting intentions, energized the atelier. The guide encouraged exploration of boundless possibilities, each intention a soul's brushstroke.

The scene became a cosmic dance of intention and creation, with the forge acting as a manifestation conduit. Alex, recognizing their thoughts' impact, embraced creation with responsibility.

In the forge, intentions took form, orchestrating a cosmic energy symphony. The guide, their words resonating like incantations, spoke of creation's interconnected nature.

Reaching a crescendo, Alex completed crafting intentions, each a truest desire reflection. The guide, acknowledging this, pointed to the next journey phase—the ethereal artists who would illuminate the path ahead.

Leaving the forge, Alex carried consciously crafted intentions, following the guide to the luminous palette—an ethereal canvas where intentions would gain vibrant life in the ongoing cosmic creation.

In the uncharted realms, Alex met the ethereal artists, collective beings shaping reality through their creative intentions. The cosmic winds hummed with their harmonious creations, and the guide, a silent observer, invited Alex into the creation dance.

The ethereal artists, glowing with creative energy, welcomed Alex. Each, a unique intention custodian, contributed to the cosmic symphony's grand tapestry.

The guide explained the artists' interconnectedness. "In

The Edge of Tomorrow

this collective dance, each intention is a cosmic melody note. Together, you shape creation's narrative."

Joining an artist, Alex learned their creative process nuances. The artist invited Alex to join the intentions dance.

Sharing creation stories, the artists conveyed collaboration's significance and subtle cosmic influences. The guide, translating cosmic languages, helped Alex grasp the creative energies.

The atelier became a vibrant intentions tableau, where thoughts transformed into reality's hues. Alex, now part of the dance, saw the beauty in individual intentions harmonizing with the collective creation pulse.

The guide highlighted the collaborative nature of ethereal creation. "Each intention adds to the shared narrative. In this dance, you are both dancer and choreographer."

As the scene climaxed, Alex, enriched by the artists' wisdom, felt connected to the cosmic symphony. The guide, understanding, led them to the luminous palette, where intentions would take vivid form on tomorrow's canvas.

The atelier, a fleeting but impactful interlude, imprinted on Alex's consciousness. Its echoes in the cosmic winds reminded Alex of the creative energies integral to self-discovery. Following the guide to the luminous palette, the artists continued their cosmic tapestry dance.

In a surreal meadow, Alex found the luminous palette, an ethereal canvas where intentions became vibrant colors. The guide, a celestial masterpiece custodian, shared wisdom on choosing resonating hues with the self's truest essence.

The meadow exuded tranquility, and the floating palette

rippled with infinite possibilities. Each color symbolized an intention aspect, from bold aspirations to nuanced desires shaping the journey.

The guide explained each hue's vibrational frequency, resonating with Alex's core. "Choose with intention," they advised, "as each color will mark tomorrow's canvas."

Approaching the palette, Alex saw a symphony of colors. The guide helped select hues harmonizing with intentions from the cosmic forge and the ethereal atelier dance.

The palette reflected Alex's inner landscape, each intention brushstroke radiating authenticity. The guide, mentoring silently, urged Alex to trust their instincts, choosing soul-song echoing colors.

Selecting colors, Alex merged memories of the journey into a cohesive narrative. The palette, a surreal creation, represented the interconnected cosmic journey threads.

As Alex painted intentions, the meadow pulsed with creative energy. The guide observed as Alex infused the canvas with truest intentions, transforming it into a testament to intentional artistry.

The palette, adorned with chosen hues, glowed transcendentally. The guide spoke of conscious creation's power, "The canvas is a living testimony to your intentions' artistry. Embrace the emerging beauty when painting with your truest self's colors."

With the canvas of tomorrow painted, Alex gazed at their creation. The meadow, a creative sanctuary, held the cosmic dance echoes—each color a harmonious intention interplay.

Stepping forward, the guide pointed to the cosmic

The Edge of Tomorrow

horizon. The palette, a catalyst for the choices symphony, set the stage for the unfolding chapters, ready for Alex to embrace the vibrant uncharted realms tapestry.

At the cosmic horizon, where realms' energies converged in a captivating display, Alex stood ready to engage in the unfolding narrative, guided by the intentions crafted in the forge, learned from ethereal artists, and painted on the luminous palette. The guide, a creation journey companion, pointed to the unveiled horizon, symbolizing endless possibilities.

The horizon rippled with destiny whispers, holding unrevealed destinies. The guide, wisdom-reflecting, spoke of this moment's significance—the culmination of intentions shaping tomorrow's landscape.

"Behold the cosmic horizon," the guide intoned. "Here, your journey's echoes harmonize with vast possibilities. Step forward, for tomorrow's canvas, now unveiled, awaits your intentions' imprints."

Approaching the horizon, Alex felt an awe sense. Charged with transformation potential, the guide, a cosmic dance anchor, accompanied them across the threshold into the uncharted territories of self-discovery.

The horizon, once a mystery, stood as a conscious choices testament made along the journey. Each step toward the unveiled expanse was an intention step—a self-discovery uncharted territories step.

The guide indicated this moment as a transition, moving from creation's preparatory stages to intentions' actualization. "Tomorrow's canvas," they said, "is shaped by your choices' brushstrokes. Embrace the unfolding chapters with an open heart to the cosmic currents."

Crossing the threshold, Alex was enveloped by horizon energies, a cosmic embrace. The guide, blending with the astral currents, became a cosmic winds whisper—a journey's fabric guide.

The scene unfolded with Alex at intention and destiny's nexus. The cosmic horizon, a potentialities tableau, resonated with creative energies. The guide, encouragingly nodding, signaled the continuing odyssey—an ongoing symphony where each choice would reverberate through time.

As the chapter closed, the cosmic horizon became infinite possibilities' portal. Carrying intentionally crafted vibrancy, Alex ventured forward into the uncharted realms, prepared to embrace the vibrant tapestry. The guide, cosmic wisdom guardian, merged into the cosmic tapestry, leaving behind guidance echoes in the cosmic winds.

Tomorrow's canvas, revealed at the cosmic horizon, awaited Alex's choices' strokes. With the guide's silent blessing, the journey continued—a cosmic odyssey where intention vibrancy continued shaping the unfolding narrative in the uncharted realms' vast expanse.

{ 7 }

Chapter 7: The Symphony of Choices

At the celestial crossroads, Alex stood in contemplation. Divergent paths stretched into the uncharted realms, and the astral currents whispered tales of undiscovered horizons. The cosmic winds seemed to carry echoes of choices yet to be made. The guide, now subtly woven into the fabric of the astral tapestry, stood beside Alex as a beacon amidst the cosmic currents.

The celestial crossroads represented an ethereal nexus where the threads of intention and destiny intertwined. The guide, their eyes reflecting the wisdom of ages, spoke of the transformative potential of each path. "Here, at the crossroads, the symphony of choices resonates through the cosmos. Each path promises revelations and challenges. Choose with intention, for the uncharted realms await your exploration."

Alex surveyed the paths, contemplating their divergent directions. The guide's words became a gentle current in the cosmic winds, reminding Alex that every step held significance in their self-discovery narrative. The crossroads felt like a sacred threshold, a convergence of myriad possibilities where intentions would shape the journey's unfolding chapters.

With a knowing smile, the guide gestured towards the paths, radiating with cosmic energies. "The journey is a dance between intention and destiny. Each choice contributes to the tapestry of your existence. Embrace this symphony of choices, for it is in choosing that you shape your cosmic narrative."

Anticipation and contemplation mingled within Alex as they considered the paths into the uncharted realms. The guide, in tune with the soul's subtle currents, encouraged Alex to trust their instincts and choose a path that resonated with their truest self.

The celestial crossroads, glowing in astral light, transformed into a tableau of possibilities. Fortified by their journey so far, Alex decisively stepped onto one of the paths. The cosmic winds, acknowledging the choice, carried the echoes of intention into the uncharted realms.

The scene closed with Alex, guided by the subtle currents of intention, walking into the cosmic horizon. The celestial crossroads, now etched into the astral tapestry, symbolized a new chapter's initiation—a chapter where choices would become melodies in the symphony of self-discovery. The guide, though a spectral presence in the astral currents, continued to walk alongside as a silent companion in the cosmic narrative.

The Edge of Tomorrow

In the heart of the uncharted realms, where destiny's whispers were carried by cosmic winds, Alex ventured deeper into ethereal landscapes. The celestial breeze, laden with subtle harmonies, seemed to guide their path, and the astral currents pointed towards unseen revelations.

The guide, now a voice in the cosmic breeze, spoke of the nuances in destiny's whispers. "The cosmic winds' dance holds your guidance. These whispers reveal your path's subtle threads, weaving through self-discovery's fabric."

Alex attuned their senses to the ethereal currents, finding clarity in the whispers. The guide, perceptive to unseen rhythms, interpreted this cosmic language—a tapestry of energies narrating the unfolding destiny story. Each whisper echoed choices made at the crossroads, intentions from the cosmic forge, and ethereal artists' collaborative dance.

The scene became a cosmic dialogue between Alex and the forces shaping their journey. The guide's voice, a constant presence, encouraged Alex to listen with their heart, reminding them that destiny's whispers resonated at intention and cosmic current intersections.

Guided by the whispers, Alex navigated ethereal meadows and cosmic glades, each step in sync with destiny's currents. The guide pointed towards a luminescent path, indicating the whispers held unfolding revelations' key.

In the uncharted depths, Alex embraced destiny's symbiotic dance. The guide echoed cosmic harmonies, speaking of interconnectedness in the unfolding narrative. "Destiny is a dynamic interplay of choices and cosmic currents. Let the whispers guide you, but your intention shapes the direction."

The scene closed with Alex, guided by celestial whispers, continuing into the uncharted realms' heart. The astral currents, now a symphonic melody, carried destiny's echoes into the cosmic winds. The guide, a spectral companion, guided Alex towards revelations beyond the next cosmic veil.

In a mystical glade within the uncharted realms, Alex found themselves at serendipity's intersection—a convergence orchestrated by destiny's unseen hands. The glade pulsed with cosmic energies' subtle harmony, and the guide, a silent witness to serendipity's dance, stood amidst the ethereal beauty, ready to share hidden moments' lessons.

Bathed in astral energy's soft luminescence, the glade presented serendipitous encounters. Alex, in tune with the cosmic symphony, recognized interconnected event threads, unfolding like a choreographed dance. Each serendipitous moment, a cosmic alignment synchronicity, whispered hidden meanings and unseen forces.

The guide, understanding cosmic intricacies, spoke of serendipity's transformative potential. "In these cosmic alignment moments, you see the universe's artistry. Serendipity is intention and destiny's subtle orchestration, inviting pattern recognition in your journey."

Alex moved through the glade, experiencing serendipitous encounters—a meeting with an ethereal creature, a convergence leading to a hidden path discovery, and moments where cosmic winds whispered upcoming opportunities. The guide, a sage in serendipity's realm, helped Alex decipher these chance encounters' language.

The scene became a serendipity tapestry meditation—a

living canvas where cosmic energy strokes contributed to the self-discovery narrative. The guide, echoing celestial melodies, spoke of these moments' interconnectedness, highlighting serendipity as not mere coincidence but a cosmic symphony sacred dance.

Embracing serendipity's dance, Alex felt deep gratitude. The glade, a transient space, held cosmic alignment echoes—a reminder of destiny's unseen hands woven into the journey.

The guide, with an understanding nod, gestured towards the continuing path. "Serendipity is a guidepost in the uncharted realms. Trust the dance, for in these moments, the universe reveals its artistry. The journey unfolds with each step, nudged gently by cosmic currents."

The scene closed with Alex, now attuned to serendipity's harmonies, continuing through the mystical glade. The cosmic winds whispered undiscovered realms' secrets, with the guide, a silent witness, accompanying the ongoing serendipity dance—a dance illuminating the uncharted landscapes with unforeseen moments' beauty and hidden revelations.

At the celestial crossroads, where divergent paths stretched into uncharted realms, Alex stood in deep contemplation. The astral currents whispered tales of undiscovered horizons, while the cosmic winds seemed to carry echoes of choices yet to be made. The guide, now a guardian of revelations, stood beside Alex, subtly woven into the astral tapestry.

The celestial crossroads was an ethereal nexus where threads of intention and destiny intertwined. The guide, their eyes reflecting ancient wisdom, spoke of the transformative potential inherent in each path. "Here, at the crossroads," they said, "the symphony of choices resonates through the cosmos. Each path you choose holds revelations and challenges. Choose with intention, for the uncharted realms await your exploration."

As Alex surveyed the paths, the guide's words became a guiding current amidst the cosmic winds, reminding them that each step had significance in their narrative of self-discovery. The crossroads, a convergence of myriad possibilities, was a sacred threshold where intentions would shape the unfolding chapters.

The guide, smiling knowingly, gestured towards the paths emanating with cosmic energies. "The journey," they said, "is a dance between intention and destiny. Each choice contributes to the expanding tapestry of your existence. Embrace this symphony of choices, for it is in choosing that you shape your cosmic narrative."

With contemplation and anticipation, Alex considered the paths leading into the uncharted realms. The guide, attuned to the soul's subtle currents, encouraged them to trust their instincts and choose a path resonating with their truest self.

The celestial crossroads, glowing in astral light, transformed into a tableau of potential. Fortified by their journey's experiences, Alex confidently stepped onto a chosen path. As they did, the cosmic winds seemed to affirm their choice, carrying the intention's echoes into the uncharted realms.

The scene closed with Alex, guided by the subtle currents

of intention, venturing into the cosmic horizon. The celestial crossroads, now a memory in the astral tapestry, symbolized the start of a new chapter, where choices would become melodies in the ongoing symphony of self-discovery. The guide, though a spectral presence in the astral currents, continued to accompany Alex, a silent companion in the cosmic narrative.

In the heart of the uncharted realms, where destiny's whispers were carried by cosmic winds, Alex journeyed deeper into ethereal landscapes. The celestial breeze, laden with destiny's subtle harmonies, seemed to guide their path, and the astral currents served as a compass toward unseen revelations.

The guide, now a voice within the cosmic breeze, spoke of the nuances in destiny's whispers. "The cosmic winds' dance," they said, "carries the guidance you seek. These whispers reveal the threads of your path, illuminating the fabric of self-discovery."

Attuning to the ethereal currents, Alex found clarity in the whispers. The guide, perceptive to unseen rhythms, interpreted the cosmic language—a tapestry of energies narrating the story of unfolding destiny. Each whisper echoed the essence of choices made at the crossroads, intentions formed in the cosmic forge, and the dance with ethereal artists.

The scene became a cosmic dialogue between Alex and the unseen forces shaping their journey. The guide's steady voice encouraged Alex to listen with the heart, reminding them that the whispers of destiny resonated at the intersection of intention and cosmic currents.

As the guiding melody of whispers became clearer, Alex found themselves navigating through ethereal meadows and cosmic glades, each step in harmony with destiny's subtle currents. The guide, a navigator in this unseen realm, pointed toward a luminescent path, hinting that the whispers held the key to future revelations.

In the uncharted depths, Alex embraced destiny's symbiotic dance. The guide, echoing cosmic harmonies, spoke of the interconnectedness of the unfolding narrative. "Destiny," they whispered, "is not a fixed path but a dynamic interplay of choices and cosmic currents. The whispers guide you, but it's your intention that shapes the direction."

The scene closed with Alex, guided by celestial whispers, continuing deeper into the uncharted realms. The astral currents, now a symphonic melody, carried destiny's echoes into the cosmic winds. The guide, a spectral companion, remained a constant guide, leading Alex toward the revelations awaiting beyond the next cosmic veil.

In a mystical glade within the uncharted realms, Alex found themselves at the intersection of serendipity—a convergence of events seemingly orchestrated by destiny's unseen hands. The cosmic energies in the glade pulsed with a subtle harmony, and the guide, now a silent witness to the dance of serendipity, stood amidst the ethereal beauty, ready to impart lessons hidden within these moments.

Bathed in astral energies' soft luminescence, the glade presented a tableau of serendipitous encounters. Alex, attuned to the cosmic symphony, recognized the interconnected threads of events unfolding like a choreographed dance. Each serendipitous moment, a synchronicity whispering hidden meanings and unseen forces at play.

The guide, understanding the cosmos's intricacies, spoke of serendipity's transformative potential. "In these cosmic alignment moments," they explained, "you witness the universe's artistry. Serendipity is the interplay of intention and destiny's subtle orchestration, inviting you to recognize patterns in your journey."

Moving through the glade, Alex encountered serendipitous moments—a chance meeting with an ethereal creature, a convergence of cosmic energies revealing a hidden path, and moments where cosmic winds whispered upcoming opportunities. The guide, a sage in the realm of serendipity, helped Alex decipher the language of these chance encounters.

The scene became a meditation on the tapestry of serendipity—a living canvas where each stroke of cosmic energy contributed to the narrative of self-discovery. The guide, echoing celestial melodies, emphasized the interconnectedness of these moments, showing serendipity as not mere coincidence but a sacred dance in the cosmic symphony.

Embracing serendipity's dance, Alex felt deep gratitude. The glade, a transient space, held cosmic alignment echoes—a reminder that destiny's unseen hands are intricately woven into the journey.

The guide, with a nod that carried cosmic understanding, gestured toward the continuing path. "Serendipity," they whispered, "is a guidepost in the uncharted realms. Trust the dance, for in these moments, the universe reveals its artistry.

The journey unfolds with each step, nudged gently by cosmic currents."

The scene closed with Alex, now attuned to serendipity's harmonies, continuing through the mystical glade. The cosmic winds, carrying the echoes of chance encounters, whispered secrets of undiscovered realms. The guide, a silent witness, remained a companion in the ongoing dance of serendipity—a dance illuminating the uncharted landscapes with unforeseen moments' beauty and hidden revelations.

{ 8 }

Chapter 8: The Cosmic Echoes

In the heart of the uncharted realms, Alex arrived at the Astral Nexus, a cosmic crossroads where the universe's energies converged in a mesmerizing display. The guide, now a spectral presence within these astral currents, stood beside them as a silent guardian of this celestial junction.

The Astral Nexus, pulsating in the glow of cosmic energies, echoed with the resonance of choices made at earlier crossroads. The guide, their eyes brimming with age-old wisdom, pointed towards the swirling cosmic winds around them. "Welcome to the Astral Nexus," they said, their voice echoing in the astral currents. "This is where your journey's echoes converge, revealing new pathways."

Alex, gazing into the cosmic expanse, felt a profound connection with their past choices' threads. The guide, a custodian of cosmic wisdom, spoke about this celestial crossroads' significance, where heartfelt intentions intersect with the forces shaping destiny.

"Every choice leaves an imprint in the astral currents," the guide continued. "Here, you can sense your journey's resonance, the decisions' echoes rippling through your existence. Contemplate these converging energies, for they weave the tapestry of your cosmic narrative."

At the Astral Nexus, Alex was surrounded by cosmic winds telling tales of the past—a symphony of echoes narrating pivotal choices. The guide, in tune with these subtle harmonies, encouraged Alex to embrace their journey's reflections, acknowledging the embedded lessons.

The scene turned into a cosmic meditation, with Alex absorbed in the Astral Nexus's energies. The guide, transcending physical presence, remained a steadfast companion in this cosmic junction. The past's echoes became a guiding force, directing contemplation of new possibilities in the uncharted realms.

As the astral winds carried these echoes forward, the guide pointed to the pathways branching from the Nexus. "Here, at the intersection of echoes and intentions, you hold the power to shape unwritten chapters. The Astral Nexus is a potential nexus, guiding the way with cosmic echoes."

The scene closed with Alex, now attuned to the Astral Nexus's energies, poised to explore the new pathways ahead. The past choices' echoes became a compass in the uncharted realms, and the guide, though spectral, remained a silent guidepost in the cosmic odyssey—a journey shaped by past echoes and weaving tomorrow's narrative.

The Edge of Tomorrow

In the Astral Nexus's heart, Alex discovered a luminous pool, reflecting vibrant cosmic energies. The guide, interwoven with the astral currents, led them to this pool—a place where heartfelt intentions materialized as ethereal ripples.

The Resonance Pool, hovering in the cosmic expanse, vibrated with intentions' frequencies. "Behold the Resonance Pool," the guide intoned. "Here, your heart's intentions take visible form. Each ripple influences the cosmic energies shaping your path."

Approaching the pool, Alex felt anticipation and introspection. The guide, mentoring silently in cosmic intentions' dance, urged them to observe the luminous depths, witnessing their intentions' reflections and astral tapestry resonances.

This became a meditation on intention's nature. Focusing on the pool, Alex saw their intentions responding, creating vibrant ripples, each echoing a heartfelt aspiration.

The guide discussed personal will's interconnectedness with cosmic currents. "In the Resonance Pool, your intentions become echoes shaping the narrative. The cosmic energies respond to your heart's desires, creating an intention-response dance."

Engaging with the pool, Alex saw their intentions as a kaleidoscope of colors—a visual symphony reflecting their inner complexities. The guide encouraged recognizing conscious intention's power.

Though celestial, the pool tangibly represented intention-cosmic forces interplay. The guide, smiling knowingly, gestured towards the Nexus's branching pathways. "The Resonance Pool showcases your creative power. Your intentions, like cosmic ocean ripples, continue influencing the unfolding narrative."

As the scene concluded, Alex, reflecting on the Resonance Pool, felt connected to their set intentions. The guide, spectral yet companionable, remained a silent witness in the intention-response dance. The Astral Nexus's pathways beckoned, and Alex, heart's desires resonating, prepared to explore the uncharted realms shaped by conscious intentions' echoes.

Beyond the Resonance Pool, Alex entered the Celestial Harmonics in the Astral Nexus—a realm where cosmic energies transformed into audible symphonies resonating through astral currents. The guide, now a figure in the cosmic tapestry, pointed to the surrounding ethereal melodies.

The Celestial Harmonics revealed a surreal soundscape of color and sound. Each cosmic current contributed a musical note to the harmonious symphony echoing through the Nexus. The guide, a silent conductor, highlighted interpreting these cosmic melodies' importance.

"Here in the Celestial Harmonics," they whispered, "intentions and destiny's vibrational frequencies manifest as sound. Listen with your heart to discern the harmonies shaping your journey's narrative."

Immersed in celestial music, Alex heard melodies of past choices, current intentions, and guiding cosmic forces. The guide, reflecting cosmic constellations, helped Alex tune into the harmonics intricately resonating across the cosmos.

As Alex discerned the celestial melodies' nuances, each note echoed a crossroads choice, an intention from the cosmic forge, or a revelation from beyond the veil. The guide,

The Edge of Tomorrow

adept at interpreting cosmic harmonics, became a mentor in the astral currents' language.

The celestial symphony, though intangible, expressed the interconnected dance between intention and destiny. Guided by the ethereal music, Alex began to see their journey's patterns—a language revealing intention and destiny's intricate interplay.

The guide spoke of the harmonies' transformative potential. "The Celestial Harmonics unveil your journey's beauty—a symphony where each choice and intention contributes to the narrative. Embrace these harmonies as echoes of your cosmic existence."

As the scene approached its zenith, Alex stood amidst the Celestial Harmonics, attuned to the melodies shaping their odyssey. The guide, blending with astral currents, silently conducted the cosmic orchestra, guiding Alex to carry these resonances into the uncharted realms where their journey's symphony would continue to unfold.

Deep within the Astral Nexus, Alex entered a unique chamber, resonating with the echoes of pivotal past decisions. Known as the Echo Chamber, this realm was where the reverberations of previous choices converged with profound resonance. The guide, now a custodian of these echoes, accompanied Alex into this ethereal sanctuary.

The Echo Chamber unfurled as a cosmic tapestry, each thread imbued with echoes transcending time and space. The guide, their expression hinting at deep knowledge, illuminated the significance of this celestial chamber. "In the Echo Chamber, at the Astral Nexus's heart, your past choices come alive. Past lessons reverberate here, while the present echoes with the potential to sculpt your ongoing story."

Stepping into the Echo Chamber, Alex was enveloped by astral currents that carried them through defining moments of their journey. These echoes spoke of crucial crossroads, forged intentions, and embraced revelations. Each reverberation bore the emotional weight of those moments, creating a mosaic of experiences within this cosmic sanctuary.

The guide, observing silently in this ethereal space, helped Alex navigate the echoes, offering insights into their interconnected nature. These reverberations became a living testament to the interplay between intention and destiny—a cosmic dialogue that unfolded in waves of energy.

In the Echo Chamber, Alex faced the echoes with introspection. Each one mirrored moments of divergent paths, intentions shaping destinies, and cosmic forces responding to heartfelt desires. The guide, gently present, encouraged Alex to extract wisdom from these echoes, recognizing how past decisions intricately shaped the present.

As Alex journeyed through this cosmic echo chamber, it became a pilgrimage through time. The guide's voice, resonating with cosmic understanding, spoke of the transformative power in embracing these echoes. "Each reverberation," they intoned, "is a growth opportunity, a chance for self-discovery. The Echo Chamber offers a space for reflection—a cosmic mirror revealing your journey's layers."

Emerging from the echoes, Alex stood at the Echo Chamber's heart, enriched by embedded lessons. The guide, though spectral, remained a silent observer—a witness to the cosmic dialogue within this ethereal sanctuary. With a newfound understanding of the echoes, Alex was ready to carry this wisdom into uncharted realms, continuing the dance between past echoes and future intentions, shaping their self-discovery narrative.

At the Astral Nexus's culmination, Alex arrived at the Threshold of Tomorrow—a mysterious cosmic portal where past echoes and future-shaping intentions converged. The guide, now a beacon towards the future, silently guarded this precipice of the unknown.

The Threshold of Tomorrow glowed with cosmic energies, casting an otherworldly aura. The guide, their gaze stretching across the astral horizon, highlighted this celestial portal's importance. "At this threshold, past echoes and present intentions merge. It's a gateway to unwritten chapters, a cosmic crossroads where intention and destiny's dance persists."

On the cosmic precipice, the tension between past choices' echoes and current intentions palpably stirred the astral currents. The guide, their words reflecting cosmic constellations, imparted final insights into the interplay between intention and destiny.

"The Threshold of Tomorrow," they whispered, "is a crossroads where past echoes guide your steps into uncharted realms. Your intentions will sculpt the unfolding narrative beyond this portal. Step through with an echo- and intention-attuned heart, for a cosmic symphony awaits."

With cosmic understanding, Alex approached the threshold. The astral currents throbbed with expectancy, and the guide, now a spectral companion, joined Alex at this critical juncture.

Crossing the cosmic portal, Alex triggered an astral currents shift. Past echoes intertwined with propelling intentions into the unknown. Though transient, the Threshold of Tomorrow initiated a new chapter where intention and destiny continued their eternal ballet.

Beyond the threshold, the uncharted realms unfurled—a cosmic landscape aglow with potential. The guide, their spectral presence now fading into the astral currents, imparted a silent blessing—a reminder that the journey proceeded with each intentional stride.

As the scene concluded, Alex, immersed in the uncharted realms, sensed past echoes guiding their path. Intentions set at the Threshold of Tomorrow became their compass in the cosmic expanse, directing the ongoing self-discovery narrative. The guide, now unseen, remained part of the cosmic winds, a guardian in the symphony of intention and destiny echoing through the vast expanse of the uncharted realms.

{ 9 }

Chapter 9: Whispers of Destiny

In the heart of the uncharted realms, Alex found themselves at the Ethereal Crossroads, a convergence point of cosmic energies hinting at unseen possibilities. The astral currents swirled around them, infused with the subtle harmonies of destiny and intention. The guide, a spectral presence interwoven with the ethereal crossroads, stood beside Alex as a silent companion in this cosmic juncture.

The Ethereal Crossroads emerged as a cosmic tableau, where the universe's energies intertwined in a vibrant dance of colors. Each pathway seemed to lead to unexplored dimensions. The guide, their eyes filled with ancient cosmic wisdom, gestured towards the intersections where destiny and intention met.

"Welcome to the Ethereal Crossroads," the guide announced, their voice resonating in the astral currents. "This is where destiny's whispers intertwine with the heart's intentions. It's a juncture where cosmic energies guide your path, and your choices reverberate through the uncharted realms."

As Alex traversed the crossroads, they were enveloped by a profound sense of interconnectedness. The guide, knowledgeable in cosmic wisdom, emphasized the importance of tuning into the subtle harmonies within the astral currents. "Listen to the whispers of destiny," they advised, "and let your intentions, like notes in a cosmic symphony, guide your journey's narrative."

The scene unfolded as a cosmic meditation, with Alex at the crossroads of past echoes and future possibilities. The guide, gesturing in a way that reflected the cosmic constellations, spoke of the crossroads' fluidity—a place where intentional choices shape the ongoing interplay of destiny and personal will.

Alex, reflecting on the ethereal energies, found a sense of purpose and direction. The crossroads transformed into a canvas where intentions painted the unfolding narrative's strokes. The guide, piercing through cosmic veils with their gaze, nodded in acknowledgment, affirming the sacred communion of Alex's journey through the Ethereal Crossroads.

With a last look at the converging paths, Alex prepared to delve deeper into the uncharted realms. The guide, though spectral, remained a steadfast companion—a silent guardian in the symphony of destiny and intention. The astral winds carried the whispers of the crossroads, guiding Alex towards the chapters yet to be written in their cosmic journey of self-discovery.

The Edge of Tomorrow

In the uncharted realms' heart, Alex stood before the Celestial Archives—a cosmic repository of echoes, where past choices' vibrational frequencies resonated through astral currents. The guide, an echo custodian, led Alex into this ethereal library, housing the past's resonating echoes.

The Celestial Archives unraveled as a celestial labyrinth, its corridors leading to echoes whispering tales of pivotal moments. The guide, their gaze transcending time, shed light on these cosmic vaults' importance. "Within the Archives, your journey's echoes are preserved. Each one is a testament to crossroads choices—the echoes shaping your existence's narrative."

Navigating the celestial library's corridors, Alex encountered tangible echoes. Each reverberation bore the emotional weight of its moment, creating an experiential symphony. The guide, mentoring silently in the dance of past echoes and present awareness, encouraged Alex to explore the archives with an open heart.

As Alex journeyed through the archives, they encountered echoes telling stories of crossroads, serendipitous encounters, and revelations beyond the veil. The guide, attuned to cosmic harmonies, offered insights into the embedded lessons. "Listen to the past's echoes," they urged. "Each holds wisdom from choices made—a cosmic dialogue guiding your path."

Delving deeper into the celestial labyrinth, the echoes wove a living tapestry, intricately piecing together moments that defined Alex's journey. The guide illuminated the interconnected threads binding intention and destiny. The echoes, remnants of the past, held power to influence both present and future.

In a quiet alcove, the guide paused, inviting Alex to reflect on a particularly resonant echo. The scene became a meditation on the interplay of intention and destiny echoes—a cosmic dialogue unfolding in energy waves.

As the scene reached its peak, Alex, enriched by the celestial vaults' lessons, prepared to rejoin the astral currents. The guide, spectral yet present, remained a silent companion—a custodian of guiding echoes. Alex, carrying new insights, ventured into the uncharted realms, where the dance of past echoes and present intentions continued to shape their journey's symphony.

In the uncharted realms' heart, Alex discovered the Celestial Forge, an ethereal workshop where intentions manifested tangibly. The guide, a guardian of creative energies, accompanied Alex, ready to share the art of shaping intentions with conscious awareness.

The Celestial Forge revealed itself as a cosmic atelier, illuminated by creative potential's luminescence. Astral currents flowed through the forge, pulsing with intentions' vibrational frequencies yet to materialize. "Welcome to the Celestial Forge," the guide intoned. "Here, intentions transcend thought; they are raw materials for the cosmos to craft your journey's narrative."

Exploring the forge, Alex felt the energies respond, weaving shimmering intention threads through the astral currents. The guide, in tune with these forces, encouraged Alex to engage in cosmic crafting. "Your intentions materialize here," they explained. "Every thought and emotion shapes the cosmos's malleable energies."

As Alex immersed themselves in creation, the forge lit up with cosmic bursts, each light manifestation bearing a heartfelt desire's essence. The guide, mentoring in cosmic creation's art, advised on infusing intentions with clarity, purpose, and resonance.

Engaging with celestial materials, Alex gained profound understanding: consciously crafted intentions form the cosmic narrative's building blocks. The forge symbolized the co-creative interplay between individual and guiding cosmic forces.

The guide, mirroring celestial constellations, spoke of intentional creation's transformative power. "The Celestial Forge reflects your ability to shape your journey. Each intention contributes to the uncharted realms' ongoing symphony."

Stepping back from the forge, Alex watched their intentions weave into the cosmic tapestry. The guide, spectral yet acknowledging, recognized the impact of intentional creation on the unfolding journey.

As the scene concluded, Alex, now aware of the forces within and around them, carried the Celestial Forge's resonance forward. The guide, a silent guardian of the creative dance, remained a companion in the narrative—a reminder that each intention shapes the cosmic symphony of self-discovery.

In the heart of the uncharted realms, Alex found themselves at the Veil of Serendipity—a cosmic shroud pulsating with chance encounters and unforeseen opportunities. The guide, adept at navigating this ethereal mist, illuminated hidden pathways within the veil, leading Alex to serendipitous moments entwined in the cosmic tapestry.

The Veil of Serendipity, a mystical mist shimmering with potential, opened doors to synchronicities, chance meetings, and revelations at each step. The guide, their eyes reflecting the cosmos's mysteries, spoke of the ethereal mist's significance.

"Here, in the Veil of Serendipity," the guide's voice melded with the astral currents, "the threads of chance and intention blend. Serendipity is where your choices meet the unexpected gifts of the cosmos."

As Alex traversed the veil, a blend of anticipation and cosmic trust enveloped them. The guide, attuned to serendipitous opportunities, urged Alex to welcome the unforeseen's dance and recognize the interconnected cosmic tapestry threads.

The scene unfolded with Alex encountering moments orchestrated by cosmic forces—kindred spirits, hidden insights, and inexplicable opportunities. The guide, smiling knowingly, highlighted pathways within the veil, each leading to serendipitous discoveries.

Within the veil, Alex found a space where intentions intersected with fate's twists. The guide, sensitive to the ethereal mist's subtleties, discussed the transformative potential in navigating this cosmic dance. "The Veil of Serendipity," they intoned, "transforms each encounter into a journey-shaping potential. Embrace the unknown for its magic in self-discovery."

Approaching the crescendo, Alex, guided by the cosmic currents, found themselves at serendipitous choices' crossroads. The guide, though spectral, silently blessed this interconnected dance of intention and surprise awaiting in the uncharted realms.

With a heart open to serendipity's dance, Alex prepared to delve further into the cosmic mist. The guide, a silent partner in the dance of chance and intention, remained a guardian as Alex continued their journey through the uncharted realms, shaped by the Veil of Serendipity's influence on their symphony of self-discovery.

At the Veil of Serendipity's culmination, Alex stood before the Threshold of Revelation—a cosmic gateway revealing hidden truths and profound realizations. The guide, now a mystery revealer, readied Alex to cross into a realm where revelations unfolded as keys to deeper self-understanding.

The Threshold of Revelation glowed with a luminescence hinting at secrets beyond. The guide, their gaze piercing the cosmic veil, highlighted this portal's importance. "At the Threshold of Revelation," they echoed, "await hidden truths and insights for those prepared to embrace journey-shaping revelations."

Before the cosmic gateway, Alex felt a mix of anticipation and inner knowing. The guide, a cosmic wisdom custodian, beckoned Alex to embrace the revelations beyond the threshold. "Cross with an open heart and seeker's spirit," they advised, "for a realm lies beyond where understanding's veils lift, revealing self-discovery mysteries."

Stepping through the portal, Alex entered a revelation realm—a landscape aglow with illuminated truths. The guide, a companion in exploring cosmic mysteries, illuminated key revelations shimmering like celestial beacons.

Revelations unveiled interconnected insights of self, cosmic forces, and the unfolding narrative. Each insight unlocked a consciousness chamber within Alex, revealing transcendent understanding layers. The guide, echoing ancient prophecies, spoke of the transformative power in embracing these threshold-emerged revelations.

Navigating through these cosmic insights, Alex attained clarity and profound knowing. The guide, revealing cosmic truths, urged Alex to integrate these insights, recognizing each as a self-awareness key.

As the scene culminated, Alex, enriched by revelations, stood beyond the threshold—a passage marking not just new realms entry but a cosmic truths awakening that shaped their journey.

Glancing back at the cosmic gateway, the guide silently acknowledged Alex's courage and curiosity leading to these revelations. Embraced by astral currents, Alex prepared to carry the illuminated truths into uncharted realms, where revelation and self-discovery's dance would continue shaping their cosmic journey's symphony.

{ 10 }

Chapter 10: The Tapestry Unveiled

In the heart of the uncharted realms, Alex entered the Cosmic Nexus, an ethereal hub where the threads of destiny converged. The astral currents around them pulsed with vibrancy, weaving through the cosmic tapestry. The guide, now a guardian of these cosmic forces, stood beside Alex, pointing out the intricate pathways weaving through the nexus.

This Nexus was a celestial mosaic, each thread a unique journey through time and space. Alex observed the luminous tapestry, where intentions, choices, and destinies vibrated together. The guide, their eyes reflecting cosmic constellations, conveyed the nexus's importance.

"Here at the Cosmic Nexus," the guide's voice harmonized with the astral currents, "destiny's threads intertwine. It's a dance between your intentions and the cosmic forces shaping your path. Attune yourself to this unfolding cosmic tapestry."

Immersed in the nexus, Alex became profoundly aware of the responsive destiny threads, shimmering with past choices' echoes and future chapters' potential. The guide, a sage of cosmic wisdom, urged Alex to sense the vibrational frequencies within the nexus, a language of interconnectedness and purpose.

As Alex considered the cosmic tapestry, they recognized intricate patterns from the interplay of intention and destiny. The guide, gesturing in tune with the cosmic dance, described the threads' fluidity—how choices made within the nexus rippled through cosmic currents, sculpting the self-discovery narrative.

At the nexus's heart, Alex felt connected to their journey's threads and countless others. The guide, sensitive to astral currents' nuances, discussed the collaborative dance of personal will and cosmic forces in destiny weaving.

Nearing its zenith, Alex stood at the crossroads of cosmic threads, engaged in the symphony of intention and destiny. The guide, though spectral, remained a steadfast guardian—a tether in the cosmic currents carrying countless journeys' resonance.

With a final look at the luminous tapestry, Alex was ready to delve deeper into the uncharted realms, armed with insights from the Cosmic Nexus. The guide, a silent companion, acknowledged the endless possibilities of self-discovery within destiny's threads.

In the Cosmic Nexus's heart, Alex engaged in Astral

The Edge of Tomorrow

Conversations—profound dialogues with ethereal beings beyond earthly understanding. The astral currents harmonized as the guide facilitated these cosmic dialogues, connecting Alex with celestial entities imparting timeless wisdom.

Alex communed with light and energy beings, each embodying cosmic consciousness. The guide bridged realms, opening channels for transcendent insights beyond human perception.

The ethereal beings shared cosmic perspectives, expanding Alex's individual consciousness. These conversations formed a collective wisdom tapestry, intertwining cosmic understanding with personal experiences. The guide, gently present, urged Alex to absorb these illuminating insights.

The astral currents echoed with these conversations. Beings discussed existence's interconnected nature, intention and cosmic force dances, and the eternal self-discovery pursuit. The guide, attuned to the dialogues, highlighted key revelations, guiding Alex through celestial discourse.

In this exchange, Alex glimpsed the cosmic tapestry's vastness—an infinite narrative woven by countless beings' intentions. The guide, smiling knowingly, emphasized interstellar conversations' significance—a reminder that self-discovery transcends earthly confines.

Reaching its zenith, Alex felt unified with cosmic forces shaping their path, enriched by collective wisdom. The guide, an interstellar dialogues guardian, silently acknowledged the gateways these celestial exchanges opened to deeper understanding.

With astral conversations' echoes in the cosmic currents,

Alex prepared to bring these insights into uncharted realms. The guide, a silent journey companion, remained a bridge between worlds—an intermediary in the cosmic symphony within the cosmic tapestry.

In the Cosmic Nexus's heart, Alex discovered the Weavers' Chamber—a celestial sanctum where cosmic entities artfully crafted destiny threads. The astral currents in this creative space pulsed with energy as the guide, overseeing these forces, invited Alex to observe the weavers' cosmic dance.

The Chamber was a transcendent workshop, glowing with iridescent threads representing intentions and destinies. Ethereal weavers moved gracefully, rhythmically intertwining cosmic threads in a dance echoing astral currents.

The guide reverently described the collaboration between personal will and cosmic forces in shaping the narrative. "In the Weavers' Chamber," they intoned, "intentions take form, destinies are woven. Observe and understand the sacred artistry that defines journeys."

Alex watched the celestial weavers craft threads with precision, each movement resonating with choices' echoes and heartfelt desires' frequencies. The guide offered insights into the weaving process—a dance harmonizing individual intentions with cosmic currents.

Alex witnessed the collaboration between weavers and cosmic forces, seeing individual intentions infused into the cosmic tapestry. The guide spoke of conscious collaboration's transformative potential in creative energies.

Reaching its zenith, Alex felt connected to the creative forces shaping destiny threads. The guide encouraged Alex

The Edge of Tomorrow

to recognize their intentions' significance in the evolving cosmic tapestry.

As the weavers completed a cosmic tapestry section, the guide gestured towards the newly woven threads. "Here," they whispered, "intentions become narrative threads. Carry this awareness beyond the sanctum."

Concluding the scene, Alex, enriched by the Chamber's insights, ventured further into the uncharted realms. The guide, a silent witness to the cosmic dance, reminded Alex that destiny's threads continued weaving through the symphony of self-discovery.

Guided by the echoes of past intentions and cosmic revelations, Alex found themselves once again at the Threshold of Tomorrow, a significant juncture in their cosmic journey. The guide, now a custodian of these echoes and revelations, stood beside Alex, ready to shed light on this pivotal moment's importance.

The Threshold of Tomorrow emanated a soft luminescence, capturing the essence of both past experiences and the boundless potential of the future. The astral currents around them hummed with the echoes of past choices, reverberating through the cosmic tapestry. The guide, with a knowing smile, elaborated on the cyclical nature of the journey, intertwining past echoes with the unknown's anticipation.

"Here at the Threshold of Tomorrow," the guide's voice resonated through the astral currents, "you stand at your journey's crossroads. Past echoes illuminate your future path. Each decision is a continuation of the cosmic dialogue that shapes your self-discovery narrative."

As Alex pondered the threshold, the guide highlighted significant echoes—an invitation to reflect on pivotal moments, revelations, and intentions that had shaped their path. The scene became a cosmic meditation, with Alex delving into echoes that spoke of resilience, growth, and the dance between personal will and cosmic guidance.

The guide encouraged Alex to see the continuity in their journey's cyclical nature. "Past echoes," they whispered, "aren't just remnants; they're threads woven through the cosmic tapestry, guiding you towards unfolding chapters."

Reflecting on these echoes, Alex felt deeply connected to their journey's narrative. The guide, emphasizing the transformative power of acknowledging these echoes, discussed the importance of learned lessons, moments of revelation, and evolving intentions in shaping the ongoing cosmic symphony.

Reaching a crescendo, Alex, enriched by insights from the Threshold of Tomorrow, felt empowered. The guide, silently affirming, acknowledged Alex's bravery in revisiting these echoes and stepping once more into the unknown.

With clarity and echoes in their heart, Alex prepared to cross the threshold, carrying past resonance into future chapters. The guide, steadfast at this cosmic crossroads, continued to accompany Alex in the dance between echoes and the unfolding cosmic forces.

On the edge of the Infinite Horizon, Alex marveled at the cosmic vista—a boundless expanse where the uncharted realms unfolded like an endless tapestry. The astral currents whispered secrets of unexplored potentialities, and the guide, a witness to the journey's evolution, stood by, imparting a final blessing.

The Infinite Horizon stretched beyond perception, a realm where destiny's threads intricately wove through the cosmic fabric. The guide, their eyes alight with distant stars' luminosity, spoke of the endless potential awaiting in the uncharted realms. "Behold the Infinite Horizon," they echoed through the cosmic winds. "Here, your journey knows no bounds, and your self-discovery narrative continually unfolds."

Gazing into the cosmic expanse, Alex felt a mix of reverence and curiosity. The astral currents carried intentions' echoes, revelations, and the creative energies of the Weavers' Chamber into this vast realm. The scene symbolized a profound realization—the journey, unbound by set paths, extended infinitely into the unknown.

The guide encouraged Alex to embrace the Infinite Horizon with an open heart. "In this expanse," they whispered, "you shape your journey. Every step paints your self-discovery canvas. Embrace the unknown, where infinite possibilities' magic lies."

Preparing to enter the uncharted realms, Alex received the guide's silent blessing, acknowledging their courage, curiosity, and resilience. The scene reflected the journey's profound interconnectedness—a dance of personal will and guiding cosmic forces.

Taking a step into the Infinite Horizon, Alex crossed into the boundless realm. The astral currents enveloped them, intertwining past echoes, revelation wisdom, and intentional weaving's creative energies. The guide, a steadfast companion at the cosmic crossroads, remained a silent anchor in the ongoing self-discovery symphony echoing through the uncharted realms' limitless expanse.

{ 11 }

Chapter 11: The Celestial Reckoning

In the Nexus of Reflection's sacred realm, Alex found themselves in a celestial sanctuary where past choices and cosmic revelations merged. The astral currents flowed gently, setting the stage for a reflective journey enriched by the uncharted realms' wisdom.

The guide, now overseeing these reflective energies, stood with Alex as they entered this nexus—a place displaying their journey's tapestry in shimmering light threads. They pointed to the center's reflective pool, its surface alive with moments etched in time's fabric.

"Welcome to the Nexus of Reflection," the guide's voice harmonized with the cosmic winds. "Here, your journey's echoes gather—a symphony of growth, challenges, and revelations. Reflect on the pivotal moments that have molded your path."

Alex peered into the pool, where their journey's scenes

played as ethereal projections. The guide gently urged Alex to delve into these memories—choices at crossroads, resilience, and revelations that unfolded in unknown realms.

This meditative journey within the nexus saw Alex navigating the reflections, each resonating with transformative power. The guide discussed acknowledging the journey's evolution, highlighting the importance of connecting past, present, and unwritten chapters. "In this nexus," they whispered, "the tapestry of self-discovery is illuminated."

Embracing the reflections, Alex felt gratitude for their journey. The guide, a silent witness to this contemplation, nodded in acknowledgment, recognizing the courage in confronting these echoes and the wisdom found in their dance.

Newly enlightened, Alex prepared to leave the Nexus of Reflection, carrying contemplation's resonance into new chapters. The guide remained a companion, anchoring the ongoing narrative of self-discovery reverberating through celestial realms.

At the Cosmic Crossroads, Alex mingled with ethereal beings personifying pivotal choices and crossroads. The astral currents hummed, resonating with otherworldly energy, as the guide facilitated encounters with these mysterious entities.

The beings shone with celestial energy, representing the diverse choices shaping the cosmic tapestry. The guide led Alex to the Cosmic Wanderer, a luminous entity embodying crossroads choices—a celestial guide through realms of decision, growth, and transformation.

"Meet the Cosmic Wanderer," the guide whispered, their

The Edge of Tomorrow

voice flowing through the astral currents. "Engage in cosmic dialogue and explore the stories that unfold."

In conversation with the Cosmic Wanderer, Alex experienced a dialogue transcending language, where intentions and cosmic forces communicated through astral vibrational frequencies. The scene wove a narrative tapestry, each being's story reflecting choice complexities and cosmic symphony impacts.

The guide, observing these celestial exchanges, introduced Alex to other entities like the Cosmic Dreamweaver and Celestial Harmonist, each offering a unique crossroads perspective.

These cosmic dialogues enlightened Alex about the interconnectedness of choices—how each decision contributes to the cosmic tapestry's symphony. The beings, timeless and transcendent, shared wisdom echoing through the astral currents.

As the scene peaked, Alex, now enriched with diverse narratives, realized each crossroad was a unique growth, transformation, and cosmic alignment opportunity.

Grateful for these cosmic encounters, Alex prepared to leave the Crossroads. The guide remained a guardian, reminding Alex that their journey continues to be shaped by the dance of personal will and guiding cosmic forces.

Before the Threshold of Renewal, Alex stood at a cosmic portal brimming with transformational energy. The astral currents in this sacred space signaled an impending profound shift. The guide, overseeing these transformative forces, readied to share insights on change's cyclical nature.

"Behold the Threshold of Renewal," they echoed through the astral currents. "Cross this portal with an open heart, signaling a rebirth of perspectives and new chapters' unfolding."

As Alex approached the threshold, the guide discussed the power of embracing change as a journey integral part. The astral currents guided Alex through the portal—a symbolic passage into a realm where old narratives gave way to new understandings.

Embracing the threshold's energies, Alex experienced a cascade of transformative forces. The guide discussed embracing change as a harmonious alignment with cosmic forces. "In every renewal," they whispered, "lies deeper self-understanding potential and cosmic harmony."

Traversing the threshold, Alex underwent a journey of surrender, shedding old narratives for a more authentic cosmic journey expression.

Emerging renewed, Alex stood transformed by the energies within the threshold. The guide acknowledged Alex's courage in embracing change, paving the way for renewal's new chapters.

Standing in the renewed cosmic landscape, the guide gestured toward the unfolding realms. The scene concluded with an understanding that renewal's cyclical dance held infinite self-discovery possibilities. Prepared with transformation's essence, Alex ventured forth into the cosmic journey's uncharted chapters.

In the Astral Symphony's heart, Alex found themselves immersed in a celestial dance—an intricate choreography of intentions and cosmic forces harmoniously flowing within the cosmic currents. The astral energies pulsed rhythmically, inviting Alex to become one with this cosmic symphony. The guide, in tune with these rhythms, stood beside Alex, encouraging them to flow with the harmonious energy movements.

"Welcome to the Astral Symphony," echoed the guide's voice, a melodic accompaniment to the celestial dance. "Here, your intentions merge with universal currents. Feel the vibrational frequencies and harmonize with the cosmic forces guiding your journey."

As Alex began moving, the astral currents responded, weaving their intentions into the cosmic dance's symphony. The scene transformed into a mesmerizing choreography, where each movement mirrored intentions, choices, and the cosmic tapestry's interconnectedness.

The guide invited celestial beings to join, embodying intentions, aspirations, and cosmic energies. The dance evolved into a collaborative expression, visualizing the interconnectedness between personal will and the universal flow.

In the Astral Symphony's heart, Alex felt unified with the guiding cosmic forces. The guide spoke of the transformative potential in aligning personal intentions with cosmic currents—a vibrant self-discovery tapestry unfolding.

As the symphony crescendoed, Alex moved with profound interconnectedness awareness in the cosmic dance. The guide, overseeing these cosmic rhythms, pointed to the evolving patterns in the astral currents, a visual representation of intentions shaping the ongoing narrative.

With a final cosmic dance swirl, the guide silently

acknowledged Alex. The astral currents subsided, leaving Alex in post-symphony stillness. The scene closed with a profound connection sense—a recognition that intention dance held transformative magic in the cosmic journey.

Prepared to carry the cosmic dance resonance, Alex stood ready for the unfolding chapters. The guide, witnessing the harmonious choreography, remained a silent guardian, reminding Alex that personal will and cosmic forces continued guiding their steps into uncharted realms.

At the chapter's culmination, Alex reached the Tapestry Unbound—a celestial finale where destiny threads converged in a breathtaking display. The astral currents within this cosmic tapestry glowed otherworldly, illuminating the intricate patterns across the vast expanse. The guide, overseeing this cosmic culmination, stood with Alex, ready to unveil the woven revelations.

"Behold the Tapestry Unbound," the guide's voice echoed through the astral currents. "Here, destiny threads converge, reflecting past echoes, transformative choices, and renewed intentions. Witness the unbound narrative's beauty unfolding before you."

Alex marveled at the celestial tapestry, where myriad threads told their journey's chapters. The guide highlighted patterns representing an intricate dance of intentions, challenges, and revelations shaping the cosmic narrative.

As a cosmic revelation, the guide unveiled the tapestry stories. Reflection echoes, Cosmic Crossroads dialogues, Threshold of Renewal transformative energies, and the

The Edge of Tomorrow

Astral Symphony harmonious dance all merged in this celestial panorama.

"The Tapestry Unbound encapsulates your journey," the guide poetically explained. "Each thread is a self-discovery moment, a made choice, and the guiding cosmic forces. Its unbound beauty symbolizes your narrative's infinite potential."

Alex traced the threads, feeling awe and gratitude. The guide, a cosmic culmination custodian, spoke of the tapestry's interconnectedness—each choice, challenge, and revelation contributing to self-discovery's unfolding chapters.

The guide invited Alex to touch the threads, to feel the vibrational frequencies within. As Alex's fingertips grazed the luminous threads, they experienced a resonating energy surge—a cosmic continuity, growth, and journey expansion affirmation.

As the scene neared its peak, the guide silently blessed Alex—a recognition of the past chapters and the boundless horizons ahead. The Tapestry Unbound became a timeless tableau, affirming the ever-evolving self-discovery journey.

With a final celestial tapestry glance, Alex stepped beyond the Tapestry Unbound, ready to explore uncharted realms. The guide, a silent cosmic narratives custodian, continued accompanying Alex in the dance between past echoes and the yet-to-reveal cosmic forces.

{ 12 }

Chapter 12: The Celestial Genesis

In the Nexus of Beginnings, Alex entered a realm where cosmic energies converged to shape new narratives. The astral currents shimmered with gentle luminescence, heralding the birth of new intentions and revelations. The guide, now a guardian of this cosmic genesis, accompanied Alex, guiding them through this sacred space.

"Welcome to the Nexus of Beginnings," echoed the guide's voice amidst celestial currents. "Here, creation's energies weave uncharted chapters. Immerse yourself in this cosmic genesis, the precursor to new narratives."

Alex, entering a state of cosmic meditation, felt the tangible energies of the nexus. Visions of celestial constellations and swirling nebulae represented limitless potential. The scene became a journey into a cosmic womb, a timeless space where intentions and revelations gestated.

The guide encouraged Alex to embrace these foundational

energies. "In the Nexus of Beginnings, intentions are seeds in the cosmic tapestry's fertile soil. Witness the raw potential preceding self-discovery chapters."

Alex, immersed in the energies, felt connected to the cosmic forces shaping their journey. The nexus became a sanctuary of introspection, nurturing intentions and awaiting revelations. The guide, understanding creation's nuances, conveyed a silent blessing, acknowledging the sacredness of this genesis.

With a final breath within the nexus, Alex prepared to step beyond, carrying beginnings' essence into uncharted realms. The guide remained a silent companion, reminding Alex that new narratives are an ongoing dialogue between personal will and cosmic guidance. As Alex ventured forth, the Nexus of Beginnings left a subtle imprint of transformative energies on their cosmic journey.

In the Cosmic Pioneers enclave, Alex encountered ethereal beings embodying exploration and pioneering spirit. The astral currents resonated with adventurous energy, and the guide facilitated celestial dialogues with these cosmic pioneers.

The beings, radiant with curiosity's spark, shared cosmic tales. The guide introduced Alex to the Cosmic Explorer, an entity embodying the courage and curiosity needed for uncharted journeys. "Meet the Cosmic Explorer," they whispered. "They embody cosmic exploration. Engage in dialogue and discover unfolding stories."

Alex's dialogue with the Cosmic Explorer transcended words, an exchange of intentions and transformative power.

The scene became a celestial symposium, offering insights into cosmic exploration and its impact on venturing into unknown realms.

The guide facilitated discussions with other pioneers, including the Cosmic Trailblazer and Nebula Voyager, each embodying aspects of cosmic exploration. Alex gained insights into the interconnected dance of intention and exploration, with wisdom echoing through the astral currents.

As the symposium peaked, Alex, enriched by diverse narratives, prepared to leave the enclave. The guide, a silent companion in exploration dialogue, remained a guardian, reminding Alex that the journey is shaped by the dance between personal will and cosmic guidance. With gratitude, Alex ventured forth, carrying the transformative energies of celestial pioneer encounters.

Before the Fountain of Intentions, Alex stood at the threshold of a celestial wellspring embodying renewed purpose and intentional weaving. The astral currents anticipated transformation, and the guide, a guardian of intentional energies, imparted wisdom on setting fresh intentions.

"Behold the Fountain of Intentions," the guide intoned. "Here, celestial waters embody renewed purpose. Infuse your intentions into the narrative."

Alex dipped their hands into the waters, symbolizing infusing the cosmic narrative with new intentions. The guide emphasized intention's role in shaping the cosmic tapestry. "Your intentions ripple through these waters, contributing to the dance of self-discovery."

Immersed in the celestial waters, Alex felt renewed. Their

intentions resonated through the cosmic tapestry, creating vibrant patterns. The guide gestured toward the evolving patterns, inviting Alex to witness their intentions' dance.

As the scene reached its peak, Alex emerged from the fountain, infused with intentional energies. The guide acknowledged the significance of this communion, recognizing its role in shaping future chapters.

Prepared to carry renewed purpose, Alex ventured forth into uncharted territories, guided by the vibrational echoes of intentional weaving, ready to shape the unfolding narrative with newfound purpose and clarity.

In the Nexus of Beginnings, Alex stepped into a realm of cosmic convergence, shaping new narratives. The astral currents glowed softly, inviting them to align with the foundational energies of new intentions and revelations. The guide, a custodian of cosmic genesis, accompanied Alex, illuminating this sacred space.

"Welcome to the Nexus of Beginnings," echoed the guide's voice amidst celestial currents. "Here, energies of creation weave uncharted chapters. Immerse yourself in this cosmic genesis, the precursor to new narratives."

Engulfed in a state of cosmic meditation, Alex felt the nexus's palpable energies. Visions of celestial constellations and swirling nebulae symbolized limitless potential. The scene became a journey into a cosmic womb, a timeless space where intentions and revelations gestated.

The guide encouraged Alex to embrace these foundational energies. "In the Nexus of Beginnings, intentions are seeds in the fertile soil of the cosmic tapestry. Witness the raw potential preceding self-discovery chapters."

Alex, immersed in the energies, felt connected to the cosmic forces shaping their journey. The nexus became an introspective sanctuary, nurturing intentions and awaiting revelations. The guide, understanding creation's nuances, conveyed a silent blessing, acknowledging the sacredness of this genesis.

With a final breath within the nexus, Alex prepared to step beyond, carrying the essence of beginnings into uncharted realms. The guide remained a silent companion, reminding Alex that new narratives are an ongoing dialogue between personal will and cosmic guidance. As Alex ventured forth, the Nexus of Beginnings left a subtle imprint of transformative energies on their cosmic journey.

In the Cosmic Pioneers enclave, Alex encountered ethereal beings embodying exploration and pioneering spirit. The astral currents resonated with adventurous energy, and the guide facilitated celestial dialogues with these cosmic pioneers.

The beings, radiant with curiosity's spark, shared cosmic tales. The guide introduced Alex to the Cosmic Explorer, an entity embodying the courage and curiosity needed for uncharted journeys. "Meet the Cosmic Explorer," they whispered. "They embody cosmic exploration. Engage in dialogue and discover unfolding stories."

Alex's dialogue with the Cosmic Explorer transcended words, an exchange of intentions and transformative power. The scene became a celestial symposium, offering insights

The Edge of Tomorrow

into cosmic exploration and its impact on venturing into unknown realms.

The guide facilitated discussions with other celestial pioneers. The Cosmic Trailblazer spoke of forging new paths through unexplored cosmic landscapes, while the Nebula Voyager resonated with the transformative energies discovered within the cosmic unknown.

In this cosmic dialogue, Alex gained insights into the interconnected dance of intention and exploration. The beings, radiant with energies that transcended time and space, imparted wisdom that echoed through the astral currents. The scene became a testament to the transformative power of embracing the unknown—a recognition that each step into uncharted territories held the potential for profound growth and self-discovery.

As the cosmic symposium reached its zenith, Alex, enriched by diverse narratives, prepared to leave the enclave. The guide, a silent companion in exploration dialogue, remained a guardian, reminding Alex that the journey is shaped by the dance between personal will and cosmic guidance. With gratitude, Alex ventured forth, carrying the transformative energies of celestial pioneer encounters.

Milton Keynes UK
Ingram Content Group UK Ltd.
UKHW020732010424
440421UK00014B/765

9 798880 532773